Northern Cardinals

Julie Murray

Abdo Kids Junior
is an Imprint of Abdo Kids
abdobooks.com

Abdo
STATE BIRDS
Kids

abdobooks.com

Published by Abdo Kids, a division of ABDO, P.O. Box 398166, Minneapolis, Minnesota 55439. Copyright © 2022 by Abdo Consulting Group, Inc. International copyrights reserved in all countries. No part of this book may be reproduced in any form without written permission from the publisher. Abdo Kids Junior™ is a trademark and logo of Abdo Kids.

Printed in the United States of America, North Mankato, Minnesota.

052021

092021

Photo Credits: Alamy, iStock, Shutterstock

Production Contributors: Teddy Borth, Jennie Forsberg, Grace Hansen

Design Contributors: Candice Keimig, Pakou Moua

Library of Congress Control Number: 2020947599

Publisher's Cataloging-in-Publication Data

Names: Murray, Julie, author.
Title: Northern cardinals / by Julie Murray
Description: Minneapolis, Minnesota : Abdo Kids, 2022 | Series: State birds | Includes online resources and index.
Identifiers: ISBN 9781098207168 (lib. bdg.) | ISBN 9781098208004 (ebook) | ISBN 9781098208424 (Read-to-Me ebook)
Subjects: LCSH: State birds--Juvenile literature. | Cardinals--Juvenile literature. | Birds--Behavior--United States--Juvenile literature.
Classification: DDC 598.297--dc23

Table of Contents

Northern Cardinals. . .4

State Bird. 22

Glossary. 23

Index 24

Abdo Kids Code. 24

Northern Cardinals

Northern cardinals live in North America.

They often live in woodlands. They are also in gardens and parks!

Males are **bright** red in color.

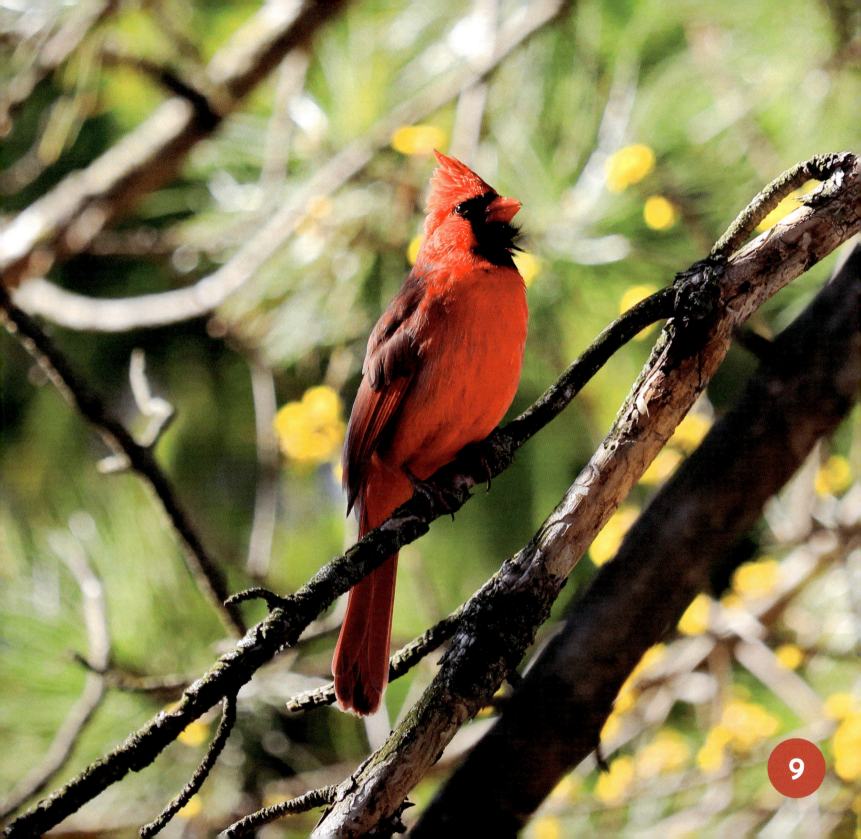

9

Females are mostly brown.

They have patches of red.

Both have **crests** on their heads.

Cardinals have orange beaks. They eat seeds and berries.

They build nests. They use leaves and twigs. The nest is in a tree or bush.

Females lay 3 to 4 eggs at a time. The eggs have dark spots.

The eggs **hatch** in 12 to 13 days. The **chicks** fly 12 days later.

State Bird

IL - Illinois   IN - Indiana   KY - Kentucky   NC - North Carolina   OH - Ohio   VA - Virginia   WV - West Virginia

Glossary

bright
strong in color.

chick
a bird that has just hatched or a young bird.

crest
a tuft of feathers on a bird's head.

hatch
to come out of an egg.

Index

beak 14

chicks 20

color 8, 10, 18

eggs 18, 20

food 14

habitat 6

head 12

markings 18

nest 16

North America 4

wings 10

Visit **abdokids.com** to access crafts, games, videos, and more!

Use Abdo Kids code **SNK7168** or scan this QR code!